This book belongs to

Isabel Patricia December 1993

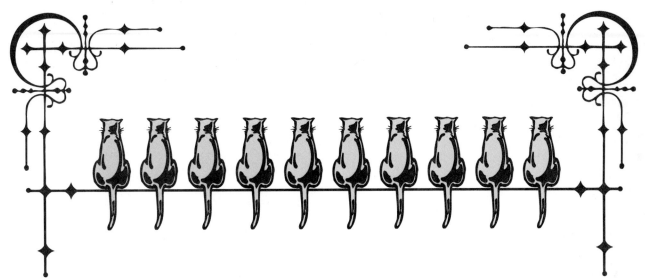

A Treasury of
Ten Tiny Tales

The Unicorn Publishing House
New Jersey

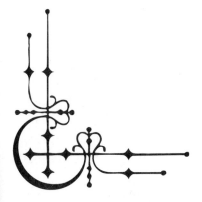
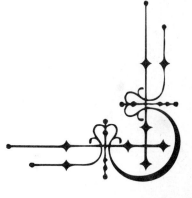

The Owl and the Pussy-Cat

I

The Owl and the Pussy-Cat went to sea
In a beautiful pea-green boat,
They took some honey, and plenty of money,
Wrapped up in a five-pound note.
The Owl looked up to the stars above,
And sang to a small guitar,
"O lovely Pussy! O Pussy, my love,
What a beautiful Pussy you are,
You are,
You are!
What a beautiful Pussy you are!"

II

Pussy said to the Owl, "You elegant fowl!

    How charmingly sweet you sing!

O let us be married! too long we have tarried:

    But what shall we do for a ring?"

They sailed away for a year and a day,

    To the land where the Bong-tree grows,

And there in a wood a Piggy-wig stood,

    With a ring at the end of his nose,

        His nose,

        His nose,

    With a ring at the end of his nose.

III

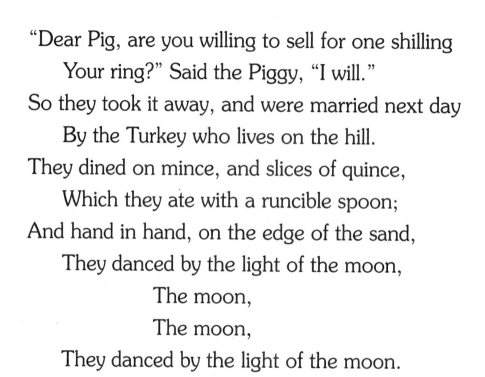

"Dear Pig, are you willing to sell for one shilling
    Your ring?" Said the Piggy, "I will."
So they took it away, and were married next day
    By the Turkey who lives on the hill.
They dined on mince, and slices of quince,
    Which they ate with a runcible spoon;
And hand in hand, on the edge of the sand,
    They danced by the light of the moon,
        The moon,
        The moon,
They danced by the light of the moon.

Wynken,
Blynken
& Nod

Wynken, Blynken, and Nod one night
Sailed off in a wooden shoe,—
Sailed on a river of crystal light
Into a sea of dew.

"Where are you going, and what do you wish?"
    The old moon asked the three.
"We have come to fish for the herring fish
    That live in this beautiful sea;
    Nets of silver and gold have we!"
              Said Wynken,
              Blynken,
              And Nod.

The old moon laughed and sang a song,
  As they rocked in the wooden shoe;
And the wind that sped them all night long
  Ruffled the waves of dew.
The little stars were the herring fish
  That lived in that beautiful sea—
"Now cast your nets wherever you wish,—
  Never afeard are we!"
  So cried the stars to the fishermen three,
            Wynken,
            Blynken,
            And Nod.

All night long their nets they threw
  To the stars in the twinkling foam,—
Then down from the skies came the wooden shoe,
  Bringing the fishermen home:
'Twas all so pretty a sail, it seemed
  As if it could not be;

And some folk thought 'twas a dream they'd dreamed
    Of sailing that beautiful sea;
    But I shall name you the fishermen three:
            Wynken,
            Blynken,
            And Nod.

Wynken and Blynken are two little eyes,
    And Nod is a little head,
And the wooden shoe that sailed the skies
    Is a wee one's trundle-bed;

So shut your eyes while Mother sings
   Of wonderful sights that be,
And you shall see the beautiful things
   As you rock in the misty sea
   Where the old shoe rocked the fishermen three:—
       Wynken,
         Blynken,
           And Nod.

The Elf and
the Dormouse

Under a toadstool
    Crept a wee Elf,
Out of the rain
    To shelter himself.

Under the toadstool,
    Sound asleep,
Sat a big Dormouse
    All in a heap.

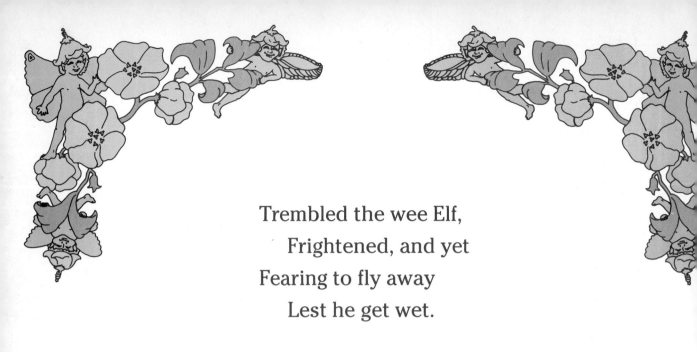

Trembled the wee Elf,
　　Frightened, and yet
Fearing to fly away
　　Lest he get wet.

To the next shelter—
　　Maybe a mile!
Sudden the wee Elf
　　Smiled a wee smile.

Tugged till the toadstool
　　Toppled in two,
Holding it over him,
　　Gaily he flew.

Soon he was safe home,
   Dry as could be.
Soon woke the Dormouse—
   "Good gracious me!

"Where is my toadstool?"
   Loud he lamented.
And that's how umbrellas
   First were invented.

Oliver Herford

The Sandman

The Sandman's coming, *soft and low,*
Coming from Sleepy Town careful and slow;
Riding on moonbeams silvery bright,
Have you ever seen such a marvelous sight!

The Sandman's coming, *soft and low,*
Bringing sweet dreams that each child knows;
Tucked in his sack, brimming with sand,
He flies through the clouds as fast as he can.

The Sandman's coming, *soft and sweet,*
When night has fallen, and it's time to sleep;
Then silently creeping close by your side,
He'll sprinkle his magic, two grains in your eyes.

Has the Sandman come to you, little one,
    Now that your busy day is done?
How will you know that he has been there—
    This clever fellow as light as air?

You will know, my dear, when first you yawn,
That, indeed, the Sandman has come and gone;
And as you rub each tired eye,
Two grains of dream sand you shall spy.

So lay your head down softly, my sweet,
And journey on to the Land of Sleep;
Snug and warm - safe from harm,
Dream sweet dreams until the dawn.

Adapted from a German Lullaby

The Pobble Who Has No Toes

I

The Pobble who has no toes
    Had once as many as we;
When they said, "Some day you may lose them all;"
    He replied,—"Fish fiddle de-dee!"
And his Aunt Jobiska made him drink,
Lavender water tinged with pink,
For she said, "The World in general knows
There's nothing so good for a Pobble's toes!"

II

The Pobble who has no toes,
    Swam across the Bristol Channel;
But before he set out he wrapped his nose,
    In a piece of scarlet flannel.
For his Aunt Jobiska said, "No harm
"Can come to his toes if his nose is warm;
"And it's perfectly known that a Pobble's toes
"Are safe,—provided he minds his nose."

III

The Pobble swam fast and well,
    And when boats or ships came near him
He tinkledy-binkledy-winkled a bell,
    So that all the world could hear him.
And all the Sailors and Admirals cried,
When they saw him nearing the further side,
"He has gone to fish, for his Aunt Jobiska's
"Runcible Cat with crimson whiskers!"

IV

But before he touched the shore,
    The shore of the Bristol Channel,
A sea-green Porpoise carried away
    His wrapper of scarlet flannel.
And when he came to observe his feet,
Formerly garnished with toes so neat,
His face at once became forlorn
On perceiving that all his toes were gone!

V

And nobody ever knew
    From that dark day to the present,
Whoso had taken the Pobble's toes,
    In a manner so far from pleasant.
Whether the shrimps or crawfish gray,
Or crafty Mermaids stole them away—
Nobody knew; and nobody knows
How the Pobble was robbed of his twice five toes!

VI

The Pobble who has no toes
    Was placed in a friendly Bark,
And they rowed him back, and carried him up,
    To his Aunt Jobiska's Park.
And she made him a feast at his earnest wish
Of eggs and buttercups fried with fish;—
And she said,—"It's a fact the whole world knows,
"That Pobbles are happier without their toes."

The Sugarplum Tree

Have you ever heard of the Sugarplum Tree?
    'Tis a marvel of great renown!
It blooms on the shore of the Lollipop Sea
    In the garden of Shut-Eye Town;
The fruit that it bears is so wondrously sweet
    (As those who have tasted it say)
That good little children have only to eat
    Of that fruit to be happy next day.

When you've got to the tree, you would have a hard time
     To capture the fruit which I sing;
The tree is so tall that no person could climb
     To the boughs where the sugarplums swing!
But up in that tree sits a chocolate cat,
     And a gingerbread dog prowls below—
And this is the way you contrive to get at
     Those sugarplums tempting you so:

You say but the word to that gingerbread dog
  And he barks with such terrible zest
That the chocolate cat is at once all agog,
  As her swelling proportions attest.
And the chocolate cat goes cavorting around
  From this leafy limb unto that,
And the sugarplums tumble, of course, to the ground—
  Hurrah for that chocolate cat!

There are marshmallows, gumdrops, and peppermint canes,
   With stripings of scarlet or gold,
And you carry away of the treasure that rains
   As much as your apron can hold!

So come, little child, cuddle closer to me
    In your dainty white nightcap and gown,
And I'll rock you away to that Sugarplum Tree
    In the garden of Shut-Eye Town.

The Rock-a-By Lady

The Rock-a-By Lady from Hushaby street
    Comes stealing; comes creeping;
The poppies they hang from her head to her feet,
And each hath a dream that is tiny and fleet—
She bringeth her poppies to you, my sweet,
    When she findeth you sleeping!

There is one little dream of a beautiful drum—
    "Rub-a-dub!" it goeth;
There is one little dream of a big sugar-plum,
And lo! thick and fast the other dreams come
Of popguns that bang, and tin tops that hum,
    And a trumpet that bloweth!

And dollies peep out of those wee little dreams
    With laughter and singing;
And the boats go a-floating on silvery streams,
And the stars peek-a-boo with their own misty gleams
And up, up, and up, where the Mother Moon beams,
    The fairies go winging!

Would you dream all these dreams—
    That are tiny and fleet?
    They'll come to you sleeping;
So shut the two eyes that are weary, my sweet,
For the Rock-a-By Lady from Hushaby street,
With poppies that hang from her head to her feet,
    Comes stealing; comes creeping.

Eugene Field

The Fairies

The Fairies are a charming folk,
     If all the tales be true,
And I believe them ev'ry one,
     And doubtless you do, too.
They live in a land enchanted,
     With their dear little Queen,
Bewitching in her loveliness,
     And dress of silv'ry sheen.

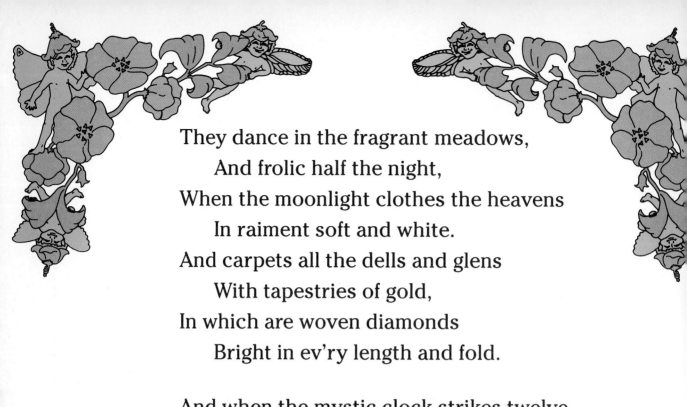

They dance in the fragrant meadows,
        And frolic half the night,
When the moonlight clothes the heavens
        In raiment soft and white.
And carpets all the dells and glens
        With tapestries of gold,
In which are woven diamonds
        Bright in ev'ry length and fold.

And when the mystic clock strikes twelve
        The Cricket's Minstrel Band,
Composed of the Court musicians,
        The greatest in the land,
Send forth its sweetest melody
        From bagpipe, flute, and horn,
In welcome to their Fairy Queen,
        The Daughter of the Morn,

Who comes, with all her maidens fair,
    To spend the night in mirth,
And dance until another day
    Is ready for its birth.
But when the light begins to fail
    In firmament above,
They bid their dainty Queen good-night
    With words of fondest love.

And then they climb the jeweled arch,
    Up through the Milky Way,
To kiss the Moon and Stars good-night
    Ere breaks the dawn of day.
Then scamper down on moonbeams pale
    Until they reach their home,
Ere God snuffs out the stars' soft light
    In heaven's matchless dome.

John G. Herndon

The Gingham Dog and the Calico Cat

The gingham dog and the calico cat
Side by side on the table sat;
'Twas half-past twelve, and (what do you think!)
Nor one nor t'other had slept a wink!
  The old Dutch clock and the Chinese plate
  Appeared to know as sure as fate
There was going to be a terrible spat.
    (I wasn't there; I simply state
    What was told to me by the Chinese plate!)

The gingham dog went "bow-wow-wow!"
And the calico cat replied "mee-ow!"
The air was littered, an hour or so,
With bits of gingham and calico,
    While the old Dutch clock in the chimney-place
    Up with its hands before its face,
For it always dreaded a family row!
        (Now mind: I'm only telling you
        What the old Dutch clock declares is true!)

The Chinese plate looked very blue,
And wailed, "Oh, dear! what shall we do!"
But the gingham dog and the calico cat
Wallowed this way and tumbled that,
    Employing every tooth and claw
    In the awfullest way you ever saw—
And, oh! how the gingham and calico flew!
    (Don't fancy I exaggerate—
    I got my news from the Chinese plate!)

Next morning, where the two had sat
They found no trace of dog or cat;
And some folks think unto this day
That burglars stole that pair away!
But the truth about the cat and pup
Is this: they ate each other up!
Now what do you really think of that!
(The old Dutch clock it told me so,
And that is how I came to know.)

The Jumblies

I

They went to sea in a Sieve, they did,
    In a Sieve they went to sea:
In spite of all their friends could say,
On a winter's morn, on a stormy day,
    In a Sieve they went to sea!
And when the Sieve turned round and round,
And every one cried, "You'll all be drowned!"
They called aloud, "Our Sieve ain't big,
But we don't care a button! we don't care a fig!
    In a Sieve we'll go to sea!"
    Far and few, far and few,
    Are the lands where the Jumblies live;
Their heads are green, and their hands are blue,
    And they went to sea in a Sieve.

II

They sailed away in a Sieve, they did,
    In a Sieve they sailed so fast,
With only a beautiful pea-green veil
Tied with a riband by way of a sail,
    To a small tobacco-pipe mast;
And every one said, who saw them go,
"O won't they be soon upset, you know!
For the sky is dark, and the voyage is long,
And happen what may, it's extremely wrong
    In a Sieve to sail so fast!"
    Far and few, far and few,
    Are the lands where the Jumblies live;
Their heads are green, and their hands are blue,
    And they went to sea in a Sieve.

III

The water it soon came in, it did,
    The water it soon came in;
So to keep them dry, they wrapped their feet
In a pinky paper all folded neat,
    And they fastened it down with a pin.
And they passed the night in a crockery-jar,
And each of them said, "How wise we are!
Though the sky be dark, and the voyage be long,
Yet we never can think we were rash or wrong,
      While round in our Sieve we spin!"
      Far and few, far and few,
      Are the lands where the Jumblies live;
Their heads are green, and their hands are blue,
    And they went to sea in a Sieve.

IV

And all night long they sailed away;
　　And when the sun went down,
They whistled and warbled a moony song
To the echoing sound of a coppery gong,
　　In the shade of the mountains brown.
"O Timballo! How happy we are,
When we live in a sieve and a crockery-jar,
And all night long in the moonlight pale,
We sail away with a pea-green sail,
　　　　In the shade of the mountains brown!"
　　　　Far and few, far and few,
　　　　Are the lands where the Jumblies live;
Their heads are green, and their hands are blue,
　　And they went to sea in a Sieve.

V

They sailed to the Western Sea, they did.
　　To a land all covered with trees,
And they bought an Owl, and a useful Cart,
And a pound of Rice, and a Cranberry Tart,
　　And a hive of silvery Bees.
And they bought a Pig, and some green Jack-daws,
And a lovely Monkey with lollipop paws,
And forty bottles of Ring-Bo-Ree,
　　　　And no end of Stilton Cheese.
　　　　Far and few, far and few,
　　　　Are the lands where the Jumblies live;
Their heads are green, and their hands are blue,
　　And they went to sea in a Sieve.

VI

And in twenty years they all came back,
    In twenty years or more,
And every one said, "How tall they've grown!
For they've been to the Lakes, and the Terrible Zone,
    And the hills of the Chankly Bore;"
And they drank their health, and gave them a feast
Of dumplings made of beautiful yeast;
And every one said, "If we only live,
We too will go to sea in a Sieve,—
      To the hills of the Chankly Bore!"
      Far and few, far and few,
      Are the lands where the Jumblies live;
Their heads are green, and their hands are blue,
    And they went to sea in a Sieve.